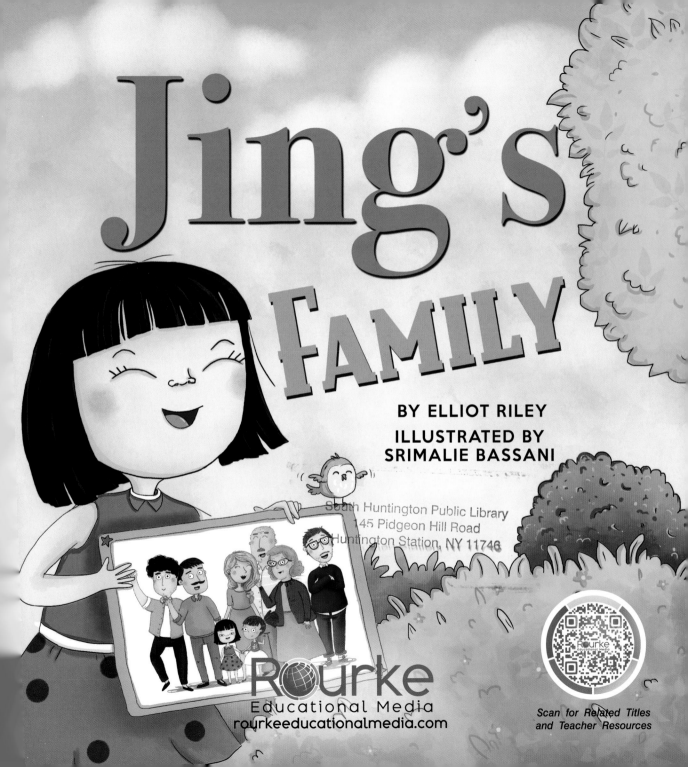

Jing's FAMILY

BY ELLIOT RILEY

ILLUSTRATED BY
SRIMALIE BASSANI

Rourke
Educational Media
rourkeeducationalmedia.com

Scan for Related Titles
and Teacher Resources

Before & After Reading Activities

Teaching Focus:
Concepts of Print: Have students find capital letters and punctuation in a sentence. Ask students to explain the purpose for using them in a sentence.

Before Reading:

Building Academic Vocabulary and Background Knowledge
Before reading a book, it is important to set the stage for your child or student by using pre-reading strategies. This will help them develop their vocabulary, increase their reading comprehension, and make connections across the curriculum.

1. Read the title and look at the cover. *Let's make predictions about what this book will be about.*
2. Take a picture walk by talking about the pictures/photographs in the book. Implant the vocabulary as you take the picture walk. Be sure to talk about the text features such as headings, the Table of Contents, glossary, bolded words, captions, charts/ diagrams, or Index.
3. Have students read the first page of text with you then have students read the remaining text.
4. Strategy Talk – use to assist students while reading.
   - Get your mouth ready
   - Look at the picture
   - Think…does it make sense
   - Think…does it look right
   - Think…does it sound right
   - Chunk it – by looking for a part you know
5. Read it again.

Content Area Vocabulary
Use glossary words in a sentence.

adopted
cousin
nearby
uncles

After Reading:

Comprehension and Extension Activity
After reading the book, work on the following questions with your child or students in order to check their level of reading comprehension and content mastery.

1. What does it mean to be adopted? (Summarize)
2. Who takes Jing to the zoo? (Asking Questions)
3. How is Jing's family like yours? How is it different? (Text to self connection)
4. What does Jing's family enjoy doing together? (Asking Questions)

Extension Activity
Trace each of your hands on a sheet of green construction paper. These will be the branches and leaves of your family tree. Write the names of all of your family members on the fingers. If you need more space, trace your hands again to make more branches. With the help of an adult, cut out each paper hand. On another piece of construction paper, draw the tree trunk. Glue the hands to the top of the trunk. Don't forget to leave some space for new family members!

Table of Contents

Meet Jing

This is Jing.

These are Jing's parents.

Jing's mom and dad **adopted** her as a baby.

She has grown a lot since then!

Play Time

Jing likes to visit her **cousin**, Anna.

Anna has two dads. They are Jing's **uncles.**

They give Jing and Anna piggyback rides.

Giddy up, uncles!

Jing's grandparents live **nearby**.

They take Jing to the zoo.

13

Jing sees many animals.

She sees many families.

Dinner Time

Jing's family cooks together.

Grandma tells funny stories.

Everyone eats and laughs.

Jing loves her family.

Jing's family loves Jing.

Picture Glossary

 **adopted** (uh-DAHPT-ed): Made a part of the family.

 **cousin** (KUHZ-in): A child of your uncle or aunt.

 **nearby** (neer-bye): A short distance away.

 **uncles** (UHNG-kuhls): The brothers of your mother or father or the husbands of your aunts.

Family Fun

Who are the people in your family?

Draw each person and write their name below their picture.

How is your family portrait like Jing's? How is it different?

About the Author

Elliot Riley is an author with a big family of her own in Tampa, Florida. She loves when everyone gets together to eat, laugh, and play games. Especially the eating part!

Meet The Author!
www.meetREMauthors.com

Library of Congress PCN Data

Jing's Family/ Elliot Riley
(All Kinds of Families)
ISBN 978-1-68342-145-0 (hard cover)
ISBN 978-1-68342-187-0 (soft cover)
ISBN 978-1-68342-217-4 (e-Book)
Library of Congress Control Number: 2016956511

Rourke Educational Media
Printed in the United States of America,
North Mankato, Minnesota

www.rourkeeducationalmedia.com

Author Illustration: ©Robert Wicher
Edited by: Keli Sipperley
Cover design and interior design by:
Rhea Magaro-Wallace

Also Available as: